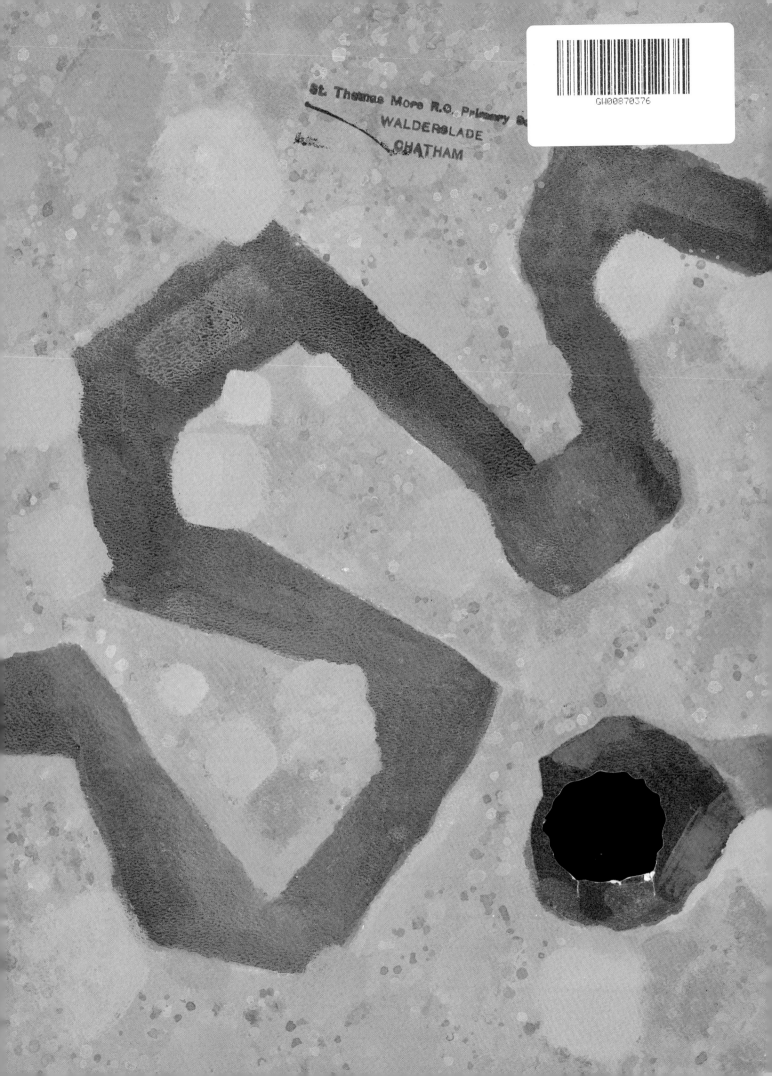

GW00870376

Ivan Gantschev

Where is Mr. Mole?

Adapted by Andrew Clements

PICTURE BOOK STUDIO

A Michael Neugebauer Book
Copyright © 1989, Neugebauer Press, Salzburg, Austria.
Published and distributed in USA by Picture Book Studio, Saxonville, MA.
Distributed in Canada by Vanwell Publishing, St. Catharines, Ont.
Published in U.K. by Picture Book Studio, Neugebauer Press Ltd., London.
Distributed in U.K. by Ragged Bears, Andover.
Distributed in Australia by Era Publications, Adelaide.
All rights reserved.
Printed in Austria by Ueberreuter

LIBRARY OF CONGRESS CATALOGING IN PUBLICATION DATA
Gantschev, Ivan.
Where is Mr. Mole?
Summary: Owl tries to track down his friend Mole who left home in search
of friendship; and though he fails to find him, Mole does turn up again
with precisely what he needs.
[1. Moles (Animals)—Fiction. 2. Animals—Fiction] I. Title.
PZ7.G15336Wh   1989   [E]   89-8778
ISBN 0-88708-109-6

Ask your bookseller for these other PICTURE BOOK STUDIO books
illustrated by Ivan Gantschev:
THE MOON LAKE
JOURNEY OF THE STORKS
THE TRAIN TO GRANDMA'S
RUMPRUMP
NOAH & THE ARK & THE ANIMALS by Andrew Clements
CANOEING by Laura Lattig
SANTA'S FAVORITE STORY by Hisako Aoki

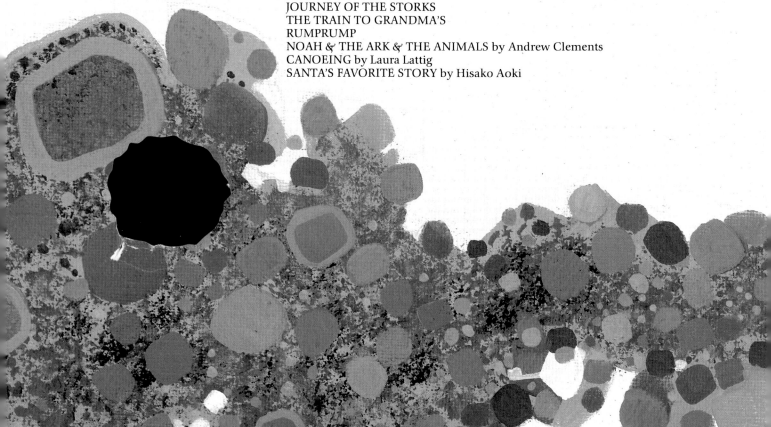

Mr. Mole had been thinking about taking a trip for a long time.
Just yesterday, he told his friend the Owl,
"I'm tired of living under the ground all alone.
I need to go out and see more of the world and make new friends
for myself."
Owl had just hooted at him, but now Mole was really ready
to leave.

"Goodbye Owl," said Mole.
"Maybe I'll be back, and maybe I won't."
After Mole was gone, Owl sat on
his rock and worried and worried
all day and all the next night, too.
Finally, Owl decided he was going to go
and be sure that Mole was all right.

Out in the meadow, Owl saw Rabbit.
"Hello, Rabbit," said Owl.
"Have you seen Mole?"

"I certainly have," said Rabbit. "He came up right in the middle of my clover patch, and invited me to come down under the ground to chew on some roots with him. When I said no, he tunneled away."

Owl stopped in a beautiful garden.
"Cat, has Mole been here?" asked Owl.
"Yes, and it was not a very pleasant visit," said Cat.
"He actually offered me a bite of a fat little worm, and said
 that he was going to stay and live right here in my garden.
 But I told him that the gardener doesn't like moles,
 so he left his worm to the hen and disappeared."

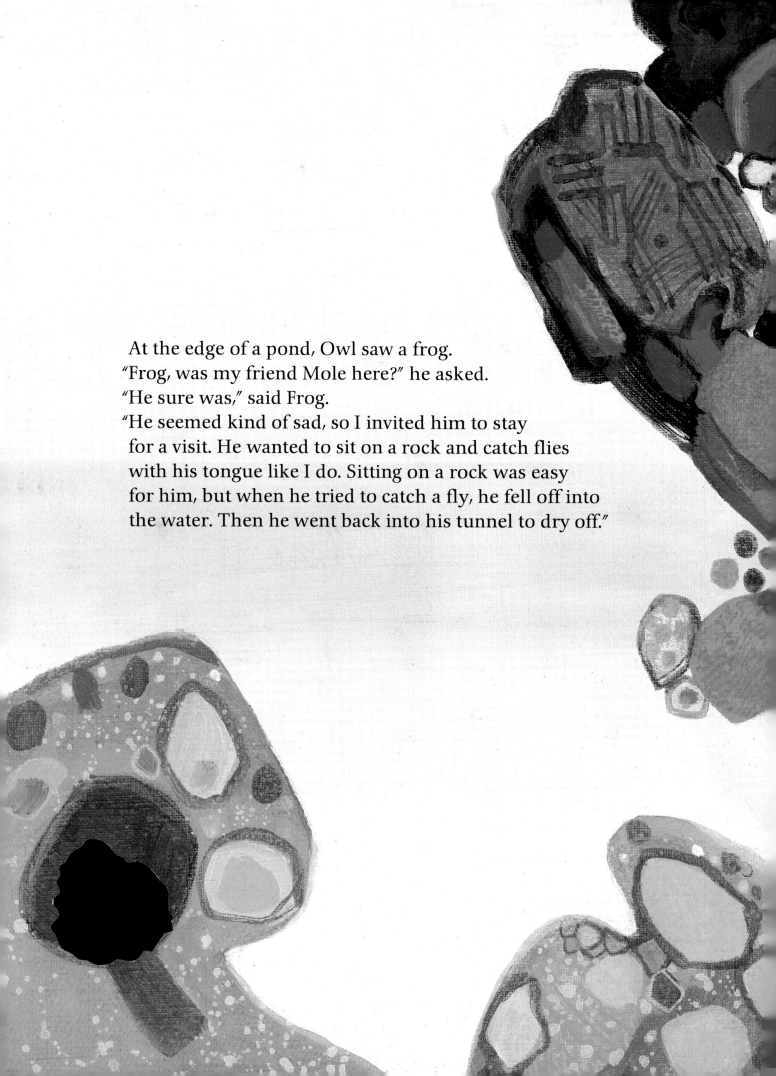

At the edge of a pond, Owl saw a frog.
"Frog, was my friend Mole here?" he asked.
"He sure was," said Frog.
"He seemed kind of sad, so I invited him to stay
for a visit. He wanted to sit on a rock and catch flies
with his tongue like I do. Sitting on a rock was easy
for him, but when he tried to catch a fly, he fell off into
the water. Then he went back into his tunnel to dry off."

By a mill stream, a fat goose was arguing with a duck.
"Mrs. Goose," interrupted Owl, "have you seen Mole?"
"Such an untidy little creature," said Goose.
"Why I just wanted to pick him up and
take him right down to the water and
give him a good scrubbing.
And I would have, too, but the miller
saw him first and started shouting
about his garden, so Mole disappeared
back into his dirty little tunnel."

Near a farm, Owl saw a fox.

"Mr. Fox, have you seen Mole?" asked Owl.

"I didn't see him," said Fox, "but I heard him go scratching by under the ground. I thought about having him for breakfast, but I had just eaten a nice plump chicken, and I wasn't hungry enough to go digging."

Owl was glad that Mole had not popped up to say hello to the fox.

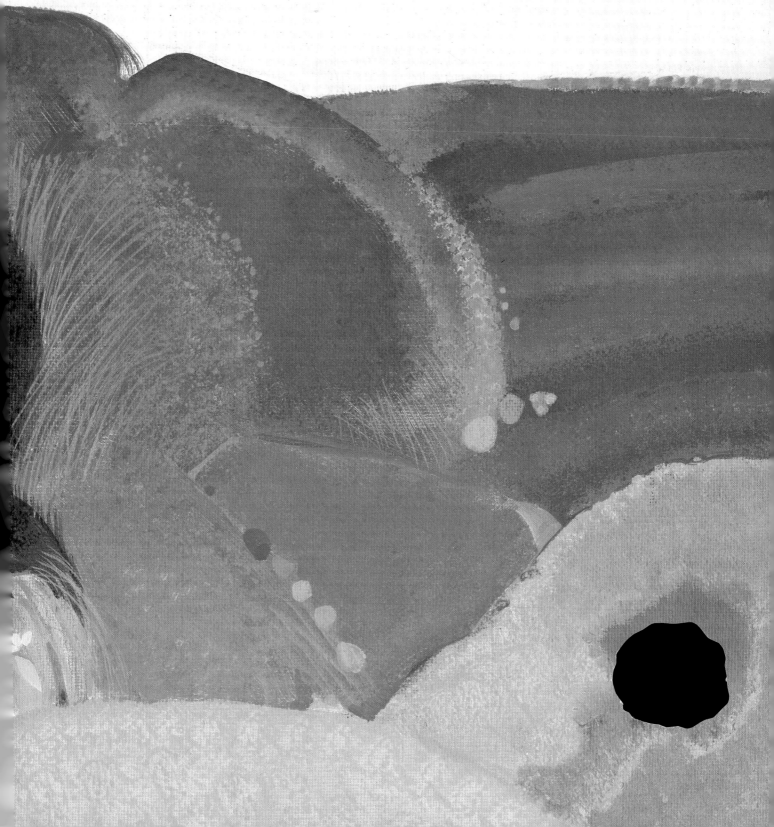

Owl came to the edge of some woods.
"Mr. Bear," asked Owl, "have you seen Mole?"
"Yes," said Bear, "he was here yesterday morning.
I invited him to climb up a tree to a beehive
and enjoy some honey with me,
but he said that he did not know how to climb trees.
Then he went back under the ground."

A sheep was standing in a pasture.
"Have you seen Mole?" asked Owl.
"Yes, he was here," said Mrs. Sheep. "He wanted to stop and talk,
but I was too busy getting ready to win a blue ribbon at the
county fair. He asked if there would be a prize for the best mole
at the fair, and when I laughed, he just left.
But he did go off in the direction of the fair."

Owl met a porcupine eating wild grapes.
"Tell me, Porcupine: Have you seen Mr. Mole?"
"Yes, he came by here about an hour ago
asking for directions to the fair.
But my mouth was full of grapes,
and he was in a hurry,
so I could only point over in that direction."
And Porcupine aimed his nose
toward the setting sun.

Owl followed Mole's trail, but instead of leading to
the fairgrounds, it went to the circus that was set up
nearby. There was so much noise and confusion,
so many bright lights and circus animals,
that Owl could not find anyone who had seen Mole.
Sadly, Owl turned around and flew back to his home.

One cold night a few weeks later Mole popped up out
of the ground and said, "Hello, Owl!"
"Well, well, well, I was beginning to think
I would never see you again," said Owl.
"Have you come back for a visit
before the snow flies?"
Mole smiled and said, "No, Owl,
I've come back home to stay,
because I found what I was looking for."

Then after a big yawn, Mole said,
"Why don't you stop over and
see me tomorrow?"

It snowed that very night, and very early the next morning
Owl visited Mole's house to see what he had found.

SHHHH...